DREAMWORKS

THE EPIC TALES OF CAPTAIN UNDERPANTS

WEDGIE POWER GUIDEBOOK

ADAPTED BY KATE HOWA

SCHOLASTIC LTD

Scholastic Children's Books,
Euston House, 24 Eversholt Street,
London NW1 1DB, UK
A division of Scholastic Ltd
London ~ New York ~ Toronto ~ Sydney ~ Auckland
Mexico City ~ New Delhi ~ Hong Kong

First published in the US by Scholastic Ltd, 2018
Published in the UK by Scholastic Ltd, 2018

Designed by Erin McMahon
Photos © Shutterstock: 8 bottom (ogieurvil), 10 background (Mavadee), 14 background and throughout (vectorplus), 17 blobs (MSSA), 19 burst and throughout (Artem Musaev), 25 bottom burst and throughout (Jo ritchy), 45 shorts (Rvector).

ISBN 978 1407 19205 5
Printed in the UK by Bell and Bain Ltd, Glasgow

2 4 6 8 10 9 7 5 3 1

www.scholastic.co.uk

CONTENTS

CHAPTER ONE:

MEET GEORGE and HAROLD

THIS IS GEORGE BEARD AND HAROLD HUTCHINS. GEORGE IS THE KID ON THE LEFT WITH THE TIE AND THE FLATTOP. HAROLD IS THE ONE ON THE RIGHT WITH THE T-SHIRT AND THE BAD HAIRCUT. REMEMBER THAT NOW.

These two pranksters are best friends and neighbors. They are also fourth graders at Jerome Horwitz Elementary School, home of the Purple Dragon Sing-A-Long Friends, where you might hear them described as:

But they are actually smart and sweet . . . and a bit silly.

SOMETIMES, THE MISCHIEF THESE TWO MAKE LEADS TO BIG TROUBLE. BUT BEFORE I CAN TELL YOU THAT STORY, I HAVE TO TELL YOU *THIS* STORY . . .

CHAPTER TWO:

GEORGE and HAROLD'S GREATEST PRANKS

GEORGE AND HAROLD *LOVE* PRANKS. SOMETIMES, THEIR JOKES ARE HARMLESS. BUT SOMETIMES, THEIR PRANKS HAVE UNEXPECTED CONSEQUENCES . . . LIKE MAKING GIANT, CRANKY VEGGIES ATTACK THE SCHOOL. BUT THAT'S A STORY FOR ANOTHER TIME.

Live by the **PRANK**, die by the **PRANK**, man!

(Wait, what's that? You can't wait? Fine. Flip to page 96.)

GEORGE AND HAROLD HAVE DONE SOME REALLY SILLY STUFF DURING THEIR TIME AT JEROME HORWITZ ELEMENTARY.

Like that time they toilet-papered Principal Krupp's car.

TP'ING THE ENTIRE SCHOOL IS GONNA BE THE GREATEST PRANK EVER.
WE'RE GONNA BE LEGENDS.

THEN THERE WAS THE TIME THEY USED THEIR

MY HAMMY SOUND MACHINE

TO HAVE SOME FUN WITH PRINCIPAL KRUPP'S MORNING ANNOUNCEMENTS.

COOL
FART MALL
AND, OF COURSE, WHO HASN'T SEEN GEORGE AND HAROLD'S CREATIVELY REARRANGED SIGNS AROUND THE SCHOOL?
erome Horwitz Elementary
SMELL YOUR
OWN
STINKY FEET
BE WARNED
WE FART SO LOUD

CHAPTER THREE: MEAN OLD MR. KRUPP

THIS IS MEAN OLD MR. KRUPP, THE MEANEST PRINCIPAL IN THE WORLD. MR. KRUPP DISLIKES KIDS . . . AND FUN. SO HE REALLY DISLIKES GEORGE AND HAROLD.

TWO TIGERS TAKE TURNS TASTING TAPIOCA. TWO TIGERS TAKE TURNS TASTING TAPIOCA.
I AM A MOUNTAIN! HOOGA!
KRUPP

EVERY TIME GEORGE AND HAROLD GET CAUGHT PLAYING PRANKS (AND ALSO THE RARE TIMES WHEN THEY AREN'T RESPONSIBLE FOR MISCHIEF), THEY GET CALLED INTO MR. KRUPP'S OFFICE.

IF YOU HIT FIVE HUNDRED VISITS TO MY OFFICE IN ONE SCHOOL YEAR, I CAN SEND YOU TO A WORK FARM WHERE YOU MILK GOATS!
VISITS
423

WE HAVE A NOTE FROM A DOCTOR.
THAT NOTE IS FROM A VET!
HOPE DIES HERE

My dogs hurt. I felt eel.
I was catatonic. My throat was horse.

CHAPTER FOUR: TREE HOUSE COMIX, INC.

WHENEVER THEY'RE NOT PLAYING PRANKS ON PRINCIPAL KRUPP, GEORGE AND HAROLD SPEND THEIR FREE TIME HANGING OUT IN THE WORLD HEADQUARTERS OF TREE HOUSE COMIX, INC. (AKA THE TREE HOUSE IN GEORGE'S BACKYARD).

INSIDE THE TREE HOUSE, THE TWO FRIENDS HAVE CREATED HUNDREDS OF COMICS STARRING SOME OF THE MOST AMAZING SUPERHEROES AND VILLAINS OF ALL TIME.

THE WORLD HEADQUARTERS OF TREE HOUSE COMIX, INC.

George writes all of the stories.
Harold illustrates them.

George and Harold love to make people laugh. And nothing makes people laugh like comics. Whenever the two pals want to figure out a funny way to deal with annoying teachers or other silly stuff, they create a new comic to solve all their problems in a hilarious way.

SOME OF THEIR GREATEST HITS INCLUDE:

CAPTAIN UNDERPANTS
AND THE DREADFUL DEBACLE of DJ DROWSY DRAWERS
DJ DROWSY
BY GEORGE BEARD

CAPTAIN UNDERPANTS
AND THE BLISTERING BLASTS OF THE BOOMING BUTTPOCOLYPSE!
TSSS
TSSS
TSSS

CAPTAIN UNDERPANTS
SINISTER FRIGHTS
SCARICA FANG

CAPTAIN UNDERPANTS
and the
FRENZIED FARTS
of
FLABBY FLAB-ULOUS
story by GEORGE BEARD
PITCHERS BY HAROLD HUTCHINS
By George Beard and Harold Hutchins

NEW HANDSHAKE!
WAIT. DOESN'T IT GO HAND, ELBOW, ARM, KNEES, TOES, AND THEN SCREAMING?
THEIR COMIC BOOKS ARE ALWAYS A HIT WITH THE OTHER KIDS . . . KIND OF LIKE FREE DONUTS OR A THREE-DOLLAR BIRTHDAY CHECK FROM AUNT CORNELIA.

GEORGE AND HAROLD HAVE MADE HUNDREDS OF HIT COMICS.
BUT EVERYONE KNOWS THAT THEIR MOST IMPORTANT CREATION
IS THE GREATEST SUPERHERO OF ALL TIME . . .

... THE ONE AND ONLY
CAPTAIN UNDERPANTS!

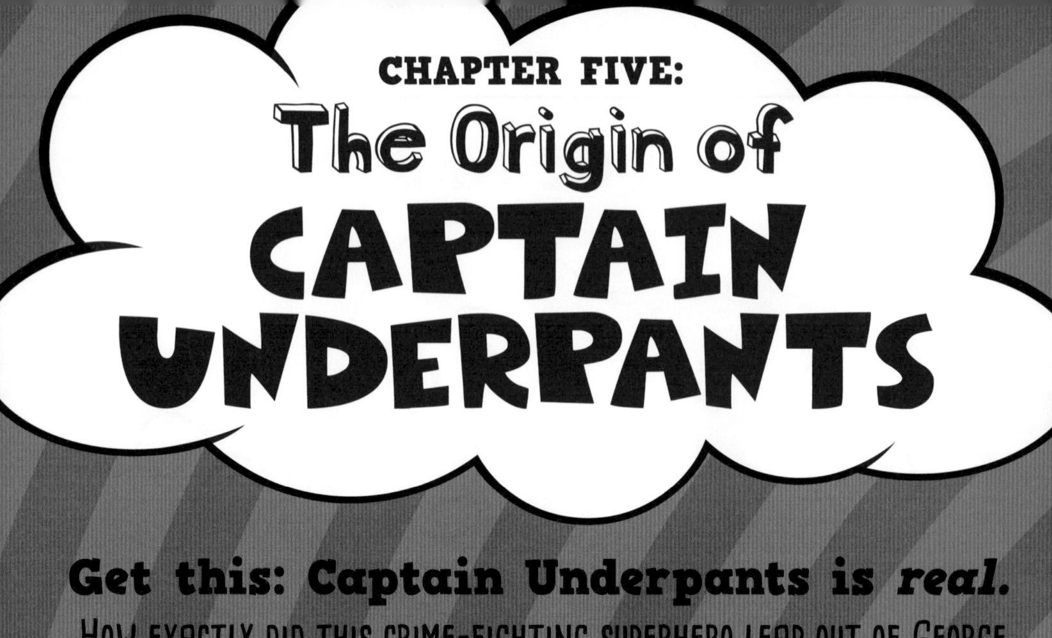

CHAPTER FIVE: The Origin of CAPTAIN UNDERPANTS

Get this: Captain Underpants is *real.*

HOW EXACTLY DID THIS CRIME-FIGHTING SUPERHERO LEAP OUT OF GEORGE AND HAROLD'S COMIC BOOKS AND COME TO LIFE? WELL, IT'S SIMPLE.

AFTER LISTENING TO MR. KRUPP YELL AT THEM ONE TOO MANY TIMES, GEORGE AND HAROLD DECIDED TO HAVE SOME FUN WITH THEIR CRANKY OLD PRINCIPAL.

Using a 3-D Hypno-Ring, they hypnotized Mr. Krupp.

At first, the boys just made him dance and had a blast watching their principal look silly. But then, they accidentally (kinda on purpose) made him believe that he was their original superhero creation: Captain Underpants.

This tighty-whitey-clad crime fighter appears whenever anyone snaps his or her fingers. When he gets splashed with water, he turns back into Principal Krupp.

Yes, that's right! With one simple snap of their fingers, all of George and Harold's problems with Mr. Krupp disappear!

SNAP!
AND CAPTAIN UNDERPANTS APPEARS.
I wear pre-shrunk cotton and they call me Cap U,
Gonna bring the noise and turn your song against you!

WITH A SNAP HE'S THE CAPTAIN
NOT THE BRIGHTEST MAN
AND DON'T FORGET
WHEN HE GETS WET
YOU'RE BACK WHERE
YOU BEGAN
(BLAH BLAH BLAH)

PUT IT ALL TOGETHER

WHAT COULD POSSIBLY GO WRONG?!

CHAPTER SIX:
MELVIN SNEEDLY and HIS INVENTIONS
Ugh! Why are you breathing like a dog?

BUT WHAT WOULD SCHOOL BE WITHOUT A KID NEMESIS? DO YOU SEE THAT KID RIGHT THERE IN THE MIDDLE OF THE FRONT ROW? THAT'S MELVIN SNEEDLY . . . HOMEWORK LOVER, INVENTOR, AND OCCASIONAL BUTT OF GEORGE AND HAROLD'S JOKES AND PRANKS.

MELVIN SNEEDLY IS VERY SMART. HE'S ALSO A GRUMPY, GRADE-GRUBBING TATTLETALE.

MELVIN'S GREATEST INVENTIONS

FROM A YOUNG AGE, MELVIN SNEEDLY DISPLAYED GREAT TALENT AT DESIGNING AND BUILDING CONTRAPTIONS BEYOND THE REACH OF MODERN SCIENCE. A FEW OF HIS BEST INVENTIONS HAVE BEEN USEFUL DURING GEORGE AND HAROLD'S PRANKS. PLUS, MELVIN'S CREATIONS HAVE ALSO COME IN HANDY – OR CAUSED SERIOUS PROBLEMS! – WHEN VILLAINS ARE ON THE LOOSE IN PIQUA.

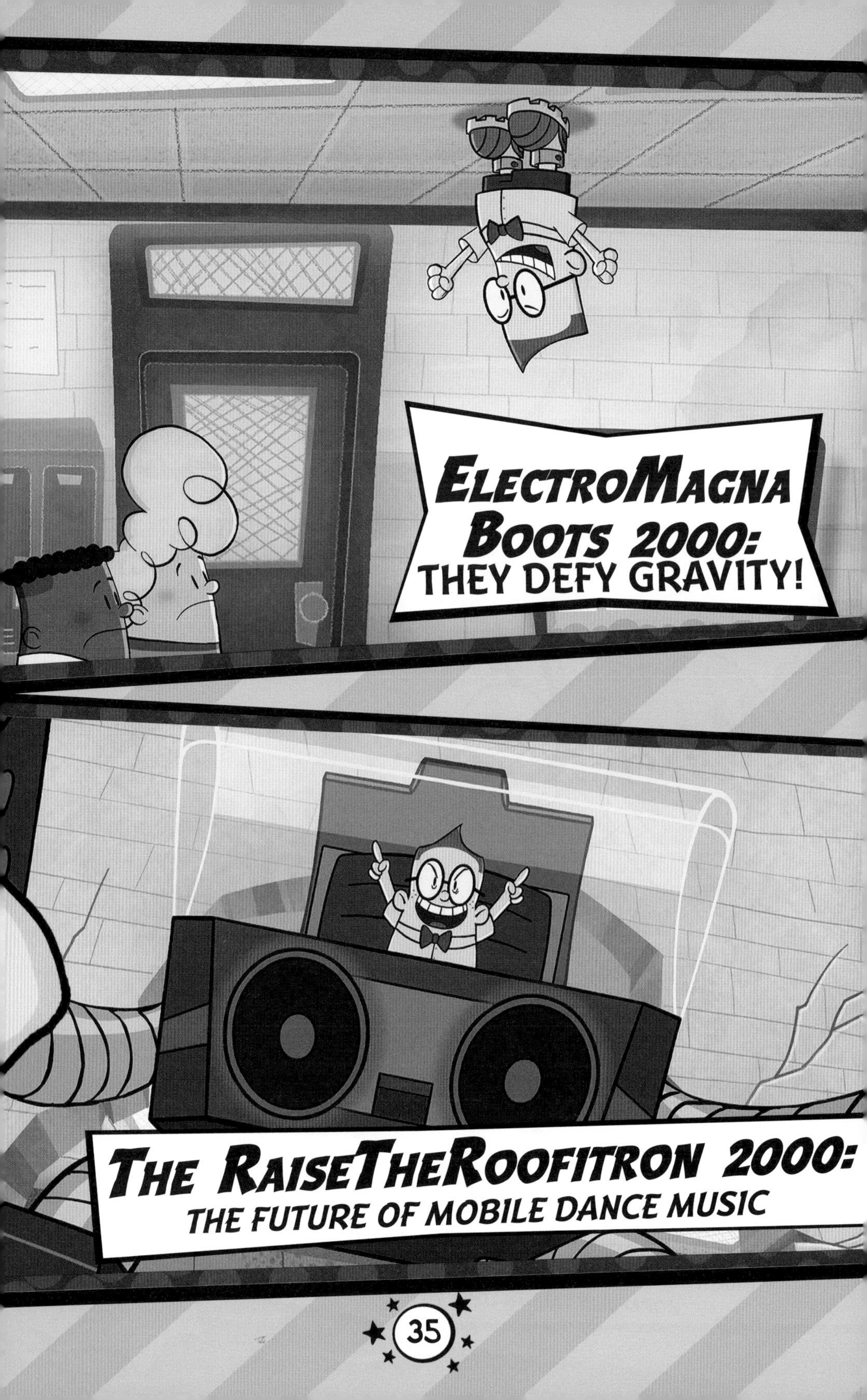
ELECTROMAGNA BOOTS 2000:
THEY DEFY GRAVITY!
THE RAISETHEROOFITRON 2000:
THE FUTURE OF MOBILE DANCE MUSIC

THE TIME TOAD 2000:
We're gonna go back in time to when homework was invented and stop it before it starts. It's that easy!
AN AMAZINGLY SOPHISTICATED PIECE OF TIME-TRAVEL TECHNOLOGY . . . POWERED BY PEANUT BUTTER.
THE BLISSKRIEG 2000:
MELVIN ORIGINALLY DESIGNED THIS HIGH-POWERED DEVICE TO BLAST HIS FAVORITE VIDEOS INTO ERICA'S BRAIN SO SHE'D THINK MELVIN IS THE BEST . . . AND HOPEFULLY FALL IN LOVE WITH HIM!
Want to know more about Erica? Turn to page 40.

THE PITACLE ACCELERATOR 2000:

All I have to do is win Avocadgrow and I'll get into Eliteanati Academy. Then the world will know my name: Melvin Sneedly. They will sing it!

THIS SNAZZY TOOL WAS DESIGNED TO HELP MELVIN WIN FIRST PRIZE IN THE SCHOOL'S AVOCADGROW COMPETITION.

CHAPTER SEVEN:

The ZANY KIDS of JEROME HORWITZ ELEMENTARY

(besides George and Harold)

JESSICA GORDON
THE SOPHIES

ERICA WANG

ERICA IS EDITOR IN CHIEF OF THE *JEROME HORWITZ EXAMINER*, LEAD SOPRANO OF THE SCIENCE SINGERS, FORMER PRESIDENT OF THE FUTURE PRESIDENTS' CLUB . . .

JESSICA GORDON

JESSICA IS FOCUSED ON ONE THING, AND ONE THING ALONE: HER AMAZING, GRAVITY-DEFYING HAIR.

Don't ruin my har!

THE SOPHIES

JESSICA'S SIDEKICKS (THAT'S ALL YOU NEED TO KNOW ABOUT THEM).

THIS FASHIONABLE FOURTH GRADER LOVES NOTHING MORE THAN SINGING AND TWIRLING HER WAY THROUGH THE DAY. SHE DESPISES PRANKS AND MISCHIEF AND EVERYTHING ELSE ANNOYING AND MESSY.

HE'S SO SWEATY HE LEAVES A SLIPPERY TRAIL BEHIND HIM.

BO IS A GIFTED SCULPTOR . . . AND DEFINITELY NOT JUST THE SCARY KID KRUPP HAS ALWAYS MADE HIM OUT TO BE.

CHAPTER EIGHT: The STRANGE STAFF of JEROME HORWITZ ELEMENTARY

MISS ANTHROPE

THE ABSENTMINDED SCHOOL SECRETARY

I VERY MUCH NEED SOME TIME OFF.

MS. HURD
THE ANCIENT, CRANKY MUSIC TEACHER (AKA DROOPY DRAWERS . . . FOR A GOOD REASON).
DID YOU KNOW . . .
THAT MS. HURD IS SO PETRIFIED OF WEREWOLVES THROWING UP THAT SHE ONCE STAYED IN HER BASEMENT FOR THREE DAYS TO AVOID THEM?
I SURVIVED BY EATING MY OWN EYELASHES AND TOENAIL CLIPPINGS!

MS. RIBBLE

THE WORLD'S MOST BORING LANGUAGE ARTS TEACHER. MOST KIDS SPEND THEIR TIME IN HER CLASS READING GEORGE AND HAROLD'S LATEST COMIC.

SEÑOR CITIZEN

THE SPANISH TEACHER WHO DOESN'T SPEAK SPANISH. HE GOT HIS JOB BECAUSE MR. KRUPP WILL HIRE *ANYONE* TO BE A TEACHER. ANYONE. EVEN WORSE, THE GUY WEARS JEAN SHORTS (AKA JORTS).

JORTS!

MR. MEANER

A GYM TEACHER ON A QUEST TO MAKE GYM CLASS EVEN WORSE THAN IT ALREADY IS.

THIS IS BRUNHILDA, THE DISGUSTING COUCH THAT LIVES INSIDE MR. MEANER'S GYM. BRUNHILDA IS *VERY* HEAVY AND HAS BEEN A MAJOR PROBLEM FOR STUDENTS SINCE FOREVER. SOME SAY BRUNHILDA CONTAINS THE MUMMIFIED BODIES OF JEROME HORWITZ ELEMENTARY'S LAST NINETY-FIVE GYM TEACHERS. OTHERS SAY IT'S JUST FULL OF COINS (WHICH IT IS).

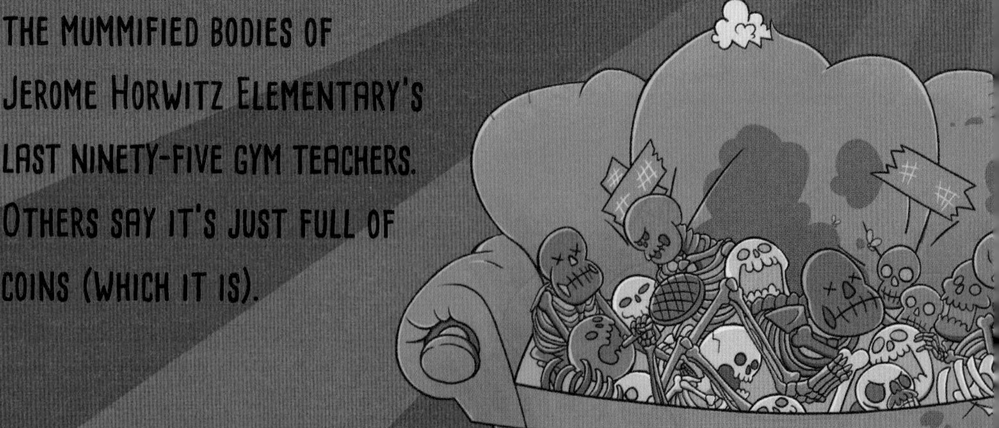

MR. FYDE

THIS AWFUL SCIENCE TEACHER SPENT SIX MONTHS RESTING IN THE PIQUA VALLEY HOME FOR THE REALITY-CHALLENGED. BUT HE'S BETTER NOW, AND READY TO TEACH SCIENCE AGAIN . . . AS LONG AS EVERYONE KEEPS THE NOISE DOWN.

MS. YEWH
THE SCHOOL'S NEW FRENCH TEACHER LOVES EVERYTHING FRENCH AND HAS ALWAYS WANTED TO GO TO PARIS. BUT SHE'D SETTLE FOR FRENCH-SPEAKING CANADA.
OOH LA LA! MS. YEWH IS AN EXCELLENT TEACHER WITH A GREAT HEAD OF HAIR AND SHE SMELLS LIKE ST. PATRICK'S DAY. LE SIGH!

MR. REE

THE SCHOOL'S JANITOR IS A DEDICATED EMPLOYEE . . . WHO DEFINITELY DOESN'T HAVE A SECRET PAST. (OOPS, I'VE SAID TOO MUCH!) HE WORKS AT THE SCHOOL BECAUSE HE GETS TO KEEP ANYTHING THAT'S BEEN LEFT IN THE LOST AND FOUND FOR MORE THAN A MONTH.

IN CASE YOU'RE CURIOUS: MR. REE USED TO BE A SECRET TOILET AGENT. THE GOVERNMENT HIRED HIM TO MAKE T.E.R.D.S.—TOILET ELIMINATOR OF REALLY DANGEROUS STUFF. T.E.R.D.S. WAS A HUGE, MASSIVE TOILET CREATED TO ELIMINATE THE MOST SERIOUS THREATS ON EARTH: POISONOUS CHEMICALS, WEAPONS OF MASS DESTRUCTION, ENVELOPES . . .

MR. RECTED

THIS MELLOW MATH TEACHER IS NEVER SEEN WITHOUT HIS BOW TIE. MR. RECTED ENJOYS THE SIMPLE THINGS IN LIFE: FRESHLY DRIED SOCKS, THE BROWNIES SERVED IN THE CAFETERIA ON THURSDAYS, AND AVOIDING CONFRONTATION AT ALL COSTS.

LUNCH LADIES

THEY MAKE AWFUL FOOD THAT IS TERRIFYING. ENOUGH SAID.

CHAPTER NINE: TREE HOUSE COMIX PRESENTS ITS GREATEST HITS

BY GEORGE BEARD AND HAROLD HUTCHINS

THE VILLAINS IN GEORGE AND HAROLD'S COMIC BOOKS HAVE BEEN KNOWN TO COME TO LIFE. (TRUST ME, IT HAPPENS FAR, FAR TOO OFTEN.)

IN THEIR QUEST TO FIND WAYS TO . . .

- ☆ **Make the school dance more exciting!**
- ☆ **Get rid of homework forever!**
- ☆ **Create a cool, kick-butt female character!**
- ☆ **(And other stuff like that)**

. . . GEORGE AND HAROLD HAVE DEVELOPED SOME OF THE COOLEST SUPER-VILLAINS IN HISTORY.

BUT AS SOON AS EACH COMIC IS FINISHED, THE BAD GUYS IN THE STORY COME TO LIFE . . . AND CAPTAIN UNDERPANTS MUST FIGHT A REAL-LIFE FOE!

Read on to meet some of Tree House Comix's most exciting creations . . .

CAPTAIN UNDERPANTS

AND THE DREADFUL DEBACLE of DJ DROWSY DRAWERS

DJ DROWSY

Once upon a time, our school was gonna have a dance. All the kids were excited because they loved dancing.

But the mean principal hated dancing.

He says, "DJ Drowsy Drawers? You're hired!"

But it was a trap! DJ Drowsy Drawers was an evil alien robot lady!

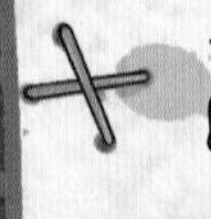

At the dance, DJ Drowsy Drawers played boring beats and did boring rap.

The kids tried to dance, but they couldn't stay awake.

Just then, Captain Underpants swooped in.

And he drank a whole bunch of soda!

But Captain Underpants fought back—for truth, justice . . .

. . . and he kinda wanted those walkie-talkies.

So he stuffed his ears with pre-shrunk cotton.
NOW I CAN'T HEAR YOU! HERE'S YOUR WAKE-UP CALL— IT'S PUNCH O'CLOCK!
DJ
DJ
DJ Drowsy Drawers swung back . . .
. . . and knocked Captain Underpants to the bottom of the page — right next to the walkie-talkies.

Captain Underpants turned up the volume on one walkie-talkie all the way. Then he threw it at DJ Drowsy Drawers, who caught it!

Then Captain Underpants took his and burped into it.

It was so loud that all the nuts and bolts popped out of DJ Drowsy Drawers. She fell to the ground in pieces.

"Hooray!" yelled everyone who was asleep. And then they all learned the Underpants Dance.

SCHOOL DANCE!

TRA-LA-LAAAAA!
THE END.

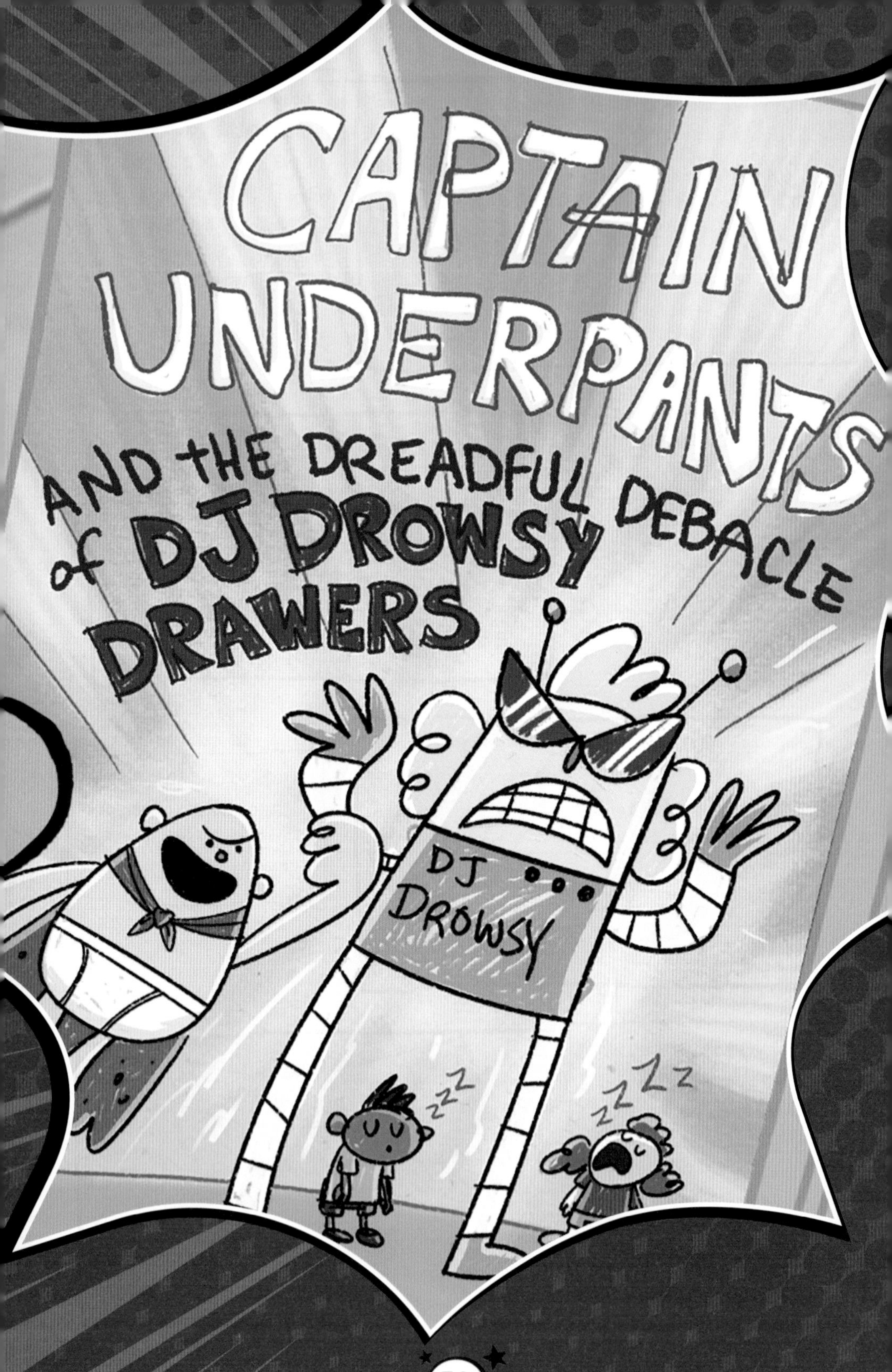

CAPTAIN UNDERPANTS

AND THE DREADFUL DEBACLE of DJ DROWSY DRAWERS

DJ DROWSY

ZZZ

ZZZZ

SO HOW, EXACTLY, DID BORING MS. HURD GO FROM DROOPY-PANTS MUSIC TEACHER TO REAL-WORLD VILLAIN WHO WREAKED HAVOC ON THE SCHOOL DANCE?
DJ Drowsy Drawers is real?!!? And here?!!? How'd that happen?
WELL, A CHEMICAL . . . ER, CAFETERIA FOOD TRUCK WAS SPEEDING TOWARD THE SCHOOL TO DELIVER NEXT WEEK'S MENU . . . AND THE TOXIC SUBSTANCE SPILLED OUT AND TURNED MS. HURD INTO DJ DROWSY DRAWERS!
SLEEEEEP! DEEEEEP!

LUCKILY, GEORGE AND HAROLD WERE ABLE TO USE MELVIN'S RAISETHEROOFITRON 2000 AND THEIR TRUSTY SUPERHERO – GOOD OL' CAPTAIN UNDERPANTS – TO SAVE THE SCHOOL FROM EVIL!

Wake up and fight!
I don't wanna wake up and fight!

SLEEP FIGHT!
TRA-LA-LAAAAA!
THE END

CAPTAIN UNDERPANTS AND George + Harold
the HEROIC HAMMERING of the HOMEWORK-HEADED HORROR!

Once there were these cool and super-buff guys, George and Harold, who did not like homework at all.

Neither did any of the other kids . . .

So the very buff guys went back in time to stop homework from being made up in the first place.

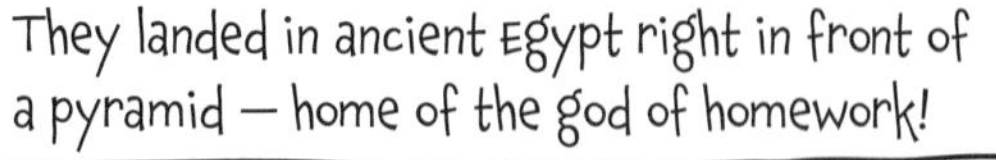

And then the god of homework turned into a hydra monster with a bunch of heads.

The Homework Hydra started to eat them.

Luckily, Captain Underpants was also in ancient Egypt on vacation. He got lost looking for the bathroom.

Buff George and Buff Harold were like, "Help and stuff! Help and stuff!"

Captain Underpants zoomed up and punched the Hydra.

He dropped Buff George and Buff Harold, who were all happy.

The Hydra reached for Buff George and Buff Harold, but Captain Underpants grabbed them just in time!

Everything smashed together, and the Hydra got knocked out.

When he woke up, he couldn't remember anything – including that he'd ever thought up the idea of homework. So he didn't invent homework after all!

CAPTAIN UNDERPANTS and the Horrible Hostilities of the Homework Hydra

SO HOW DID THE HOMEWORK HYDRA SPRING OUT OF THE PAGES OF GEORGE AND HAROLD'S COMIC BOOK AND INTO THE LIVES OF THE STUDENTS AT JEROME HORWITZ ELEMENTARY? WELL . . . IT ALL BEGAN BECAUSE EVERY TEACHER AT SCHOOL DROOLED ABOUT HOMEWORK. THEY LOVED TO MAKE STUDENTS MISERABLE.

So George and Harold came up with a plan to get rid of homework – forever. But things went a little wrong . . . and they turned their teachers into a horrifying, five-headed Homework Hydra! (Well, technically, it wasn't Mr. Meaner's head – it was his butt.)
Never fear, pre-shrunk cotton is here!
But fortunately, Captain Underpants came to the rescue!

CAPTAIN UNDERPANTS
AND THE
SINISTER FRIGHTS
OF
SCARICA FANG
story by GEORGE BEARD
PICTURES by Harold Hutchins

Once there was this strong female character named Scarica Fang.

She was a real know-it-all who sucked the joy out of everything. She was all "You're so wrong". . .

. . . and "You eat too much cheese and stuff."

Then one time this bat flew into the school and she goes, "You don't fly right."

The bat got all sad and cried — and then he bit her. He had melancholy bat venom!
I'M SCARICA FANG. I'M SO SAD AND VANT TO SUCK YOUR JOY!
And it turned her into a vimpire! Which is like a vampire, but it sucks vim, aka joy, instead of blood!
So she flew all around school biting funny bones and sucking joy!

She got bigger and stronger until she busted out of the school.
I GOT UNDERWEAR DOWN THERE! AND AN ALBINO GATOR!
Just then, Captain Underpants was leaving the Underground Underwearhouse.
I TOOK THEIR JOY, AND I WILL TAKE YOURS!
But the kids were crying and stuff.
NUH-UH! STOP IT OR ELSE!
OR ELSE NOTHING!

Captain Underpants didn't want to drop all his new underwear.
So he threw the albino gator at her, but it just stuck to her head.

IT'S ALL CLEAN AND FRESH!
YOUR ALBINO GATOR IS USELESS AGAINST ME!

So he threw all his new underwear at her.

NINJA-STYLE!

Scarica looked like an Underwear Snowman. The kids thought it was so funny they LOL'ed like crazy.

Captain Underpants was getting their joy back!

There was so much laughing that Scarica laughed, too!

Scarica got so big and round, the kids could jump on her like a bouncy house all day.

TRA-LA-LAAAAA! THE END.

CAPTAIN UNDERPANTS AND THE VEXING VILLAINY OF THE VILE VIMPIRE
SO HOW DID THE VILE VIMPIRE SPRING OUT OF THE PAGES OF GEORGE AND HAROLD'S COMIC AND INTO REAL LIFE AT JEROME HORWITZ ELEMENTARY? WELL, AFTER GEORGE AND HAROLD DECIDED TO MAKE A COMIC THAT WAS A LITTLE DIFFERENT THAN USUAL . . .
Let's make a comic *about* Erica! We'll make her the star of the comic! And we'll give her special Erica powers!

. . . THINGS WENT WRONG AS USUAL. ERICA HATED THE COMIC BOOK – AND SO DID ALL THE OTHER KIDS. AND THEN MELVIN DECIDED TO TEST HIS BLISSKRIEG 2000 ON JESSICA GORDON. WHEN HE ZAPPED HER, HE ACCIDENTALLY TURNED JESSICA INTO A *REAL* VIMPIRE WHO SUCKED THE JOY OUT OF EVERYONE AROUND HER!
I'm not Jessica Gordon anymore! I'm Messica Gorgon! And I vant to suck your JOY!
WHAT DID YOU DO TO MY HAIR?
Was that supposed to hurt? You kick like a baby!
Don't judge me, I'm also fighting my emotions! I'm just a man . . . in underpants!

CAPTAIN UNDERPANTS
And the
FRENZIED FARTS
OF
FLABBY FLAB-ULOUS
Story by GEORGE BEARD
PITCHERS BY HAROLD HUTCHINS

Once there was a skinny guy named Flabby. But he had a huge butt, and he loved it.

He thought people with small butts were missing out.

Even though Flabby was happy with his big butt, people made fun of him. They called him "Flabby Flabulous."

He liked that name and even got T-shirts made. But nobody bought them.

That made him really mad, so he went around town and crushed all the T-shirt stores.
HAT MADE HIM
REALLY MAD
NOTE
FLABBY
BOUNC

Then he crushed Captain Underpants's favorite underwear store.

But guess who was inside the store? Captain Underpants!

YOU CAN'T CRUSH BUILDINGS! ESPECIALLY UNDERWEAR STORES!
YES I CAN!
Captain Underpants tried to fight him, but he couldn't get past Flabby's big butt.

Captain Underpants pulled an extra pair of underwear from his utility waistband.

So he looked for something bigger to give Flabby Flabulous a wedgie.

Luckily, there was an underwear factory nearby. Its flagpole had a huge pair of underwear.

Captain Underpants was about to grab the underwear when Flabby made a big fart.

Captain Underpants flew back to try again, but Flabby blasted him right through the panels of the comic book!
Flabby didn't see him enter the next page . . .
. . . and Captain Underpants stuck Flabby in a huge smokestack on the factory!
CAP FLIES
CAP DROPS FLABBY

Flabby couldn't stop his fart. Finally . . .

. . . he launched into space and flew all the way to Uranus, where the aliens loved big butts and Flabby's was the biggest.

He was like a king, and so he stayed there. The end.

CAPTAIN UNDERPANTS AND THE FRENZIED FARTS OF FLABBY FLABULOUS

Now, I bet you're wondering how a comic-book villain like Flabby Flabulous ended up coming to life and attacking the town of Piqua. It all started when George and Harold decided to get back at their horrible gym teacher, Mr. Meaner, by writing him into a comic book . . .

A FEW DAYS LATER, MR. MEANER ACCIDENTALLY GOT BLASTED BY MELVIN'S PUMPITUPINATOR 2000 – AND FLABBY FLABULOUS WAS BORN!
Why does he have that scary laugh?
He's a gym teacher.

(AT THIS POINT, YOU MAY WISH TO TURN DOWN THE SMELL IN THIS BOOK.)
Get ready to be Flabby-caked!
Pfffffffffffft!
I must summon my WEDGIE POWER to defeat this villain!

Luckily, Jessica Gordon, whose hair had never done anything for anyone except Jessica Gordon, became a major player in this story. Her hair was huge (thanks to Melvin's PumpItUpinator!), and it provided a soft, strong, and safe landing for Captain Underpants!

CAPTAIN UNDERPANTS and the QUARRELSOME TYRANNY of QUEEN TOOTENFARTI

Once there was this annoying French teacher who was awful and really loved French stuff and made all the kids talk French.

One day she took the kids on a field trip in a bus and stuff.

They were all "Yay!" until they found out it was to a museum to see French junk.

But first, they had to walk through the mummy exhibit. The mummy was Queen Tootenfarti, an ancient Egyptian queen.

The sign said DON'T TOUCH THE MUMMY!!, but the teacher did anyway . . .

. . . and the mummy woke up and farted her mummy spirit into the teacher . . .

. . . and she made the *teacher* the mummy! Her face got all rotten and yucky.

She scared all the kids.

Captain Underpants flew in.

The mummy attacked, but Captain Underpants could see she was kinda sad and stuff.

So he wrapped himself in toilet paper and made her think he was her boyfriend.

He grabbed her hand. But she was a million years old, so it crushed to dust.

She attacked! She threw all this old stuff at Captain Underpants.

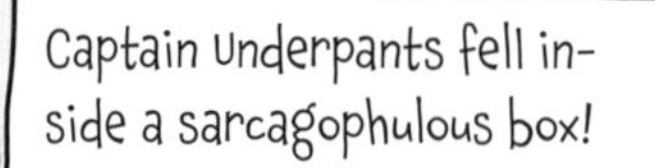

Captain Underpants fell inside a sarcagophulous box!

Tootenfarti was going to eat Captain Underpants!

But then someone hit her on the head with a frying pan and knocked her out!

And it was! It was his mum who stopped Tootenfarti and saved the day. The end.

CAPTAIN UNDERPANTS
and the Quarrelsome Tyranny of Queen Tootenfarti

SO HOW DID THE *REAL* QUEEN TOOTENFARTI END UP INVADING JEROME HORWITZ ELEMENTARY? WELL, HERE'S A GOOD ONE: WHAT DO YOU GET WHEN YOU MIX A TRUCKLOAD OF FANCY FRENCH TP AND MEGA-ULTRA-MAXIMUM-STRENGTH CLOG REMOVER WITH THE WORLD'S MOST BORING FRENCH TEACHER?

A TP MUMMY!
I am the queen! The queen of TP! Oui, oui, oui! I want all the TP! And once I have it, all will bow before me or never go to the bathroom again!
Hey, mummy! I'm gonna wipe you out. Get it? Cuz it's toilet paper!
AND THEN HE DID.

CHAPTER TEN: CAPTAIN UNDERPANTS'S GREATEST BATTLES OF ALL TIME!!

TRA-
LA-
LAAAAAA!

The Squishy Predicament of
Stanley Peet's Stinky Pits
NO NOOOOOOOISE! If you won't be quiet, I'll MAKE you quiet! I'll make the whole world quiet. FOREVER!

WHEN THINGS GOT OUT OF HAND DURING THE SCHOOL'S AVOCADGROW COMPETITION, MELVIN'S PITACLE ACCELERATOR 2000 TURNED NOISE-HATING MR. FYDE INTO GEORGE AND HAROLD'S LATEST COMIC BOOK CREATION – **AVOCADWOE!**

ONCE AGAIN, THE TOWN OF PIQUA HAS ONE MAN TO THANK FOR SAVING THEM FROM CERTAIN DOOM. CAPTAIN UNDERPANTS TO THE RESCUE!

The Costly Conundrum of the CALAMITOUS CLAYLOSSUS

AFTER LONER BO HWEEMUTH BECAME FRIENDS WITH GEORGE AND HAROLD, MELVIN UNLEASHED A NEW VILLAIN. USING HIS INTERCLAYTIONSTATION 2000, MELVIN TURNED THEIR HUGE CLASSMATE INTO CLAYLOSSUS – A VILLAIN FROM GEORGE AND HAROLD'S LATEST COMIC!

BEFORE LONG, ALL OF PIQUA HAD BEEN TURNED INTO A MOUNTAIN OF CLAY – WITH CLAYLOSSUS AS ITS RULER! LUCKILY, GEORGE AND HAROLD CONVINCED MELVIN TO REVERSE THE DYNAMICAFLOB OF THE FLOOKENSPOOGER HODANK TO TURN THE INTERCLAYTIONSTATION INTO A DEINTERCLAYTIONSTATION.

(IN NON-MELVIN TERMS: WITH CAPTAIN UNDERPANTS AND MELVIN'S HELP, GEORGE AND HAROLD WERE ABLE TO TURN CLAY BACK INTO THE SWEET, CRAFTY KID THEY HAD ALL COME TO KNOW AND LOVE.)

The Jarring Jerkiness of Judge JORTS
I FOUND THIS COOL ROBE AND IT GAVE ME POWERS! I'M A REAL SUPERHERO, JUST LIKE IN YOUR COMIC!
I AM JUDGE JORTS! JUSTICE! ORDER! RIGHTEOUSNESS! TENACITY! SHORTS!

WHEN SEÑOR CITIZEN FOUND A COOL ROBE, HE PUT IT ON SO HE COULD GET SUPER POWERS. THEN THINGS WENT VERY, VERY WRONG . . .

THE TRUTH WAS, JUDGE JORTS WAS A *TERRIBLE* SUPERHERO. HE CAUSED WAY MORE PROBLEMS THAN HE SOLVED. AND JUST WHEN THINGS GOT BAD IN PIQUA . . . THEY BEGAN TO GET MUCH, MUCH WORSE. THAT'S WHEN CAPTAIN UNDERPANTS GOT INVOLVED AND SAVED THE DAY!

The Strange Strife of the SMELLY SOCKTOPUS

WHEN A BOTTLE OF MR. KRUPP'S TOUPEE POLISH SPILLED ONTO A PILE OF DIRTY SOCKS, WELL, LET'S JUST SAY IT REALLY STANK. WHY? WELL, THE THIRD INGREDIENT IN THAT TOUPEE POLISH WAS EVIL. SO THERE YOU HAVE IT.

We gotta do something to help Captain Underpants!
Didn't Socktopus say he hates beefin' shoes?
We need a giant shoe so we can stuff him in it!
Yeah, like in our beefin' comic!

The Flustering Mindless Woe of the Flushable Memory Wipes
WHEN URINAL-CAKE SALESMAN THEODORE MURDSLY TRICKED EVERYONE AT JEROME HORWITZ INTO USING MEMORY-ERASING BUTT WIPES, HE BRAINWASHED THE WHOLE SCHOOL INTO THINKING HE WAS AMAZING . . . AND HE TRIED TO TAKE OVER THE SCHOOL!
I'LL WIPE YOUR BRAINS SO CLEAN, YOU'LL BE ABLE TO EAT OFF THEM!

LUCKILY, CAPTAIN UNDERPANTS SAVED THE DAY . . . WITH A GIANT VAT OF CHOCOLATE PUDDING. (OBVIOUSLY.)

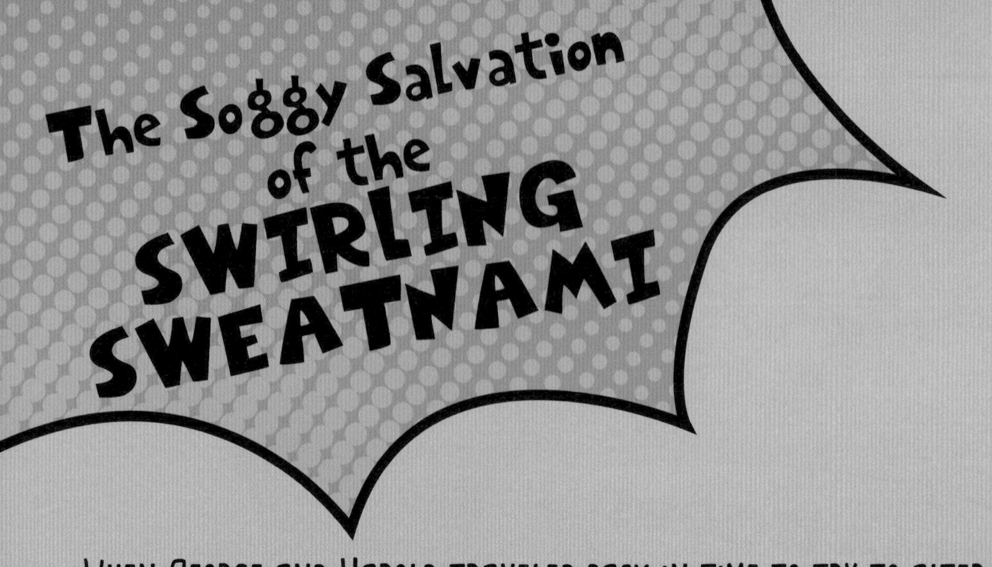

The Soggy Salvation of the SWIRLING SWEATNAMI

WHEN GEORGE AND HAROLD TRAVELED BACK IN TIME TO TRY TO ALTER THE MOMENT IN HISTORY WHEN MR. KRUPP TURNED INTO A MEAN OLD GRUMP, THINGS DIDN'T GO QUITE THE WAY THEY'D PLANNED. AND WHEN *MELVIN* GOT INVOLVED, THINGS GOT MUCH, MUCH WORSE.

It's nothing personal. I just don't like you.
AHHHH! THERE'S NOTHING QUITE LIKE SURFING AWAY FROM BAD GUYS ON A WAVE OF SWEAT.
Grab a dolphin floaty and surf your way to freedom!
SURF'S UP!
Sweatnammiiiiii!

SMARTSY FARTSY

The Sickening Fumes of the Smartsy Fartsy

MELVIN'S LATEST INVENTION, THE ELEVAPOR 2000, TURNED LIFELESS GAS INTO AN INTELLIGENT, LIVING CLOUD. SO GEORGE AND HAROLD USED IT TO MAKE GEORGE'S FART COME TO LIFE! WICKED!

It's Smartsy Fartsy from our comic! Only smart! We made him out of my fart!
YOU CAN'T FIGHT GAS!
Oh, no! I breathed him in and I taste fart!

BET YOU THOUGHT IT COULDN'T GET MUCH WORSE THAN SMARTSY FARTSY, THE STINKY GAS . . . WELL, IF THAT'S THE CASE, YOU'D BE WRONG.

SILENT . . . BUT DEADLY!

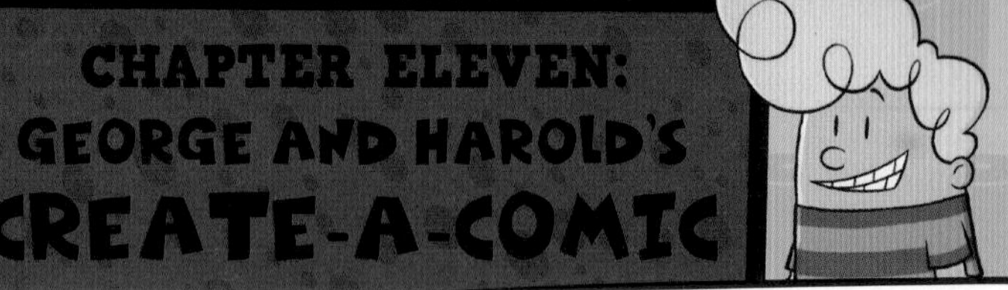

This is kiki (your first name) hyna (your last name). One day, kiki (your first name) was in Art (school subject) class when a gurgle (adjective) dude crashed (verb ending in -ed) through the door. He cried out, "Greetings, cool (adjective) fools! My name is Mr. slug (gross adjective) log (gross thing) and I am your new teacher."

kiki (your first name) had seen this gurgle (adjective) guy before! He was a wacky (adjective) villain who was trying to take over the sweeshop (place)!

"You're not a teacher!" kiki (your first name) shouted. "You are the evil villain, Professor slug (gross adjective) boggie (gross thing)!" kiki (your first name) grabbed a overly (adjective) largething (large thing) and swunged (verb ending in -ed) it at their new teacher.

But the evil villain just destroyed it (verb ending in -ed) "You can't stop me!" he yelled. "Not even that weirdo (adjective) superhero, Captain knoitedtie (article of clothing) can stop me!"

"Maybe not. But I know who can! This is a job for Captain Underpants!" kiki (your first name) cried.

"*Tra-la-laaaaa!*" yelled Captain Underpants as he To crashed (verb ending in -ed) into the room. "I am here to save all of you and your class (adjective) mates (thing ending in -s)."

He grabbed a chair (item found in a classroom) and swung it at the wacky (adjective) bad guy.

The evil villain Falled (verb ending in -ed) to the floor. "Hooray!" shouted everyone. "kiki (your first name) and Captain Underpants saved the day again!"

Reminder:

A **VERB** is an action word (like *run, hop, smash, crush,* etc.)

An **ADJECTIVE** is a word that describes a person, place, or thing (like *stinky, green, slimy, gross,* etc.)

DREAMWORKS

THE EPIC TALES OF CAPTAIN UNDERPANTS